a minedition book

Text copyright © 2003 by Brigitte Weninger
Illustrations copyright © 2003 by Robert Ingpen
First American edition, 2004
Originally published in German in 2003 by Michael Neugebauer Verlag AG, Gossau, Switzerland

Manufactured in Hong Kong by Wide World Ltd.
Designed by Michael Neugebauer
Typesetting in Veljovic, designed by Jovica Veljovic.
Color separation by Fotoreproduzioni Grafiche, Verona, Italy.

Library of Congress Cataloging-in-Publication Data available upon request.

ISBN 0-698-40007-0
10 9 8 7 6 5 4 3 2 1
First Impression
For more information please visit our website: www.minedition.com

THE MAGIC CRYSTAL

BRIGITTE WENINGER

ILLUSTRATED BY ROBERT INGPEN

TRANSLATED BY HAROLD D. MORGAN

minedition

On a beautiful mountain not far from here lived a dwarf named Pico. He was a very kind-hearted and friendly dwarf, but he was also hunchbacked and rather ugly. Pico lived all alone in a small cave. He was ashamed of how he looked, so he hid in his cave during the day so that no one would see him. When night came, Pico would go up the mountain, where he would work hard breaking stones.

From time to time a stinky old troll would come to visit
Pico. The troll would snoop around the cave nosily.
Pico would give him something to eat, and then the stinky
old troll would toddle off again without so much as a
"good-bye" or "thank you."

One night, under a full moon, as Pico climbed the mountain, he heard a soft sound. Curiously, he stopped to listen. Colorful lights glistened in the rocks. In front of a crack in the cliff, Pico saw a group of crystal dwarves. They were dancing and singing a song. And they sang it over and over and over again:

> *"The magic crystal catches the eye.*
> *It sparkles and glows like…"*

Whenever they would come to the missing rhyme, the dwarves would pause, look at each other in a puzzled way, and start the song all over again.

Pico was sorry that such a pretty song didn't have an ending. The next time through, he quietly sang along, and he finished the rhyme himself:

> "The magic crystal catches the eye.
> It sparkles and glows like the sun in the sky."

Immediately, Pico was surrounded by a group of very excited crystal dwarves. "That was beautiful!" they shouted. "You're a poet! You're a singer! You gave our song an ending. Please come with us to the Crystal King."

The crystal dwarves showed Pico the way and led him through a dark entrance that went deep into the mountain. Pico stared in amazement. He had never seen anything so beautiful. The cave was huge and full of crystals. But the most beautiful of all was the magnificent crystal in the center. It glistened with all the colors of the rainbow.

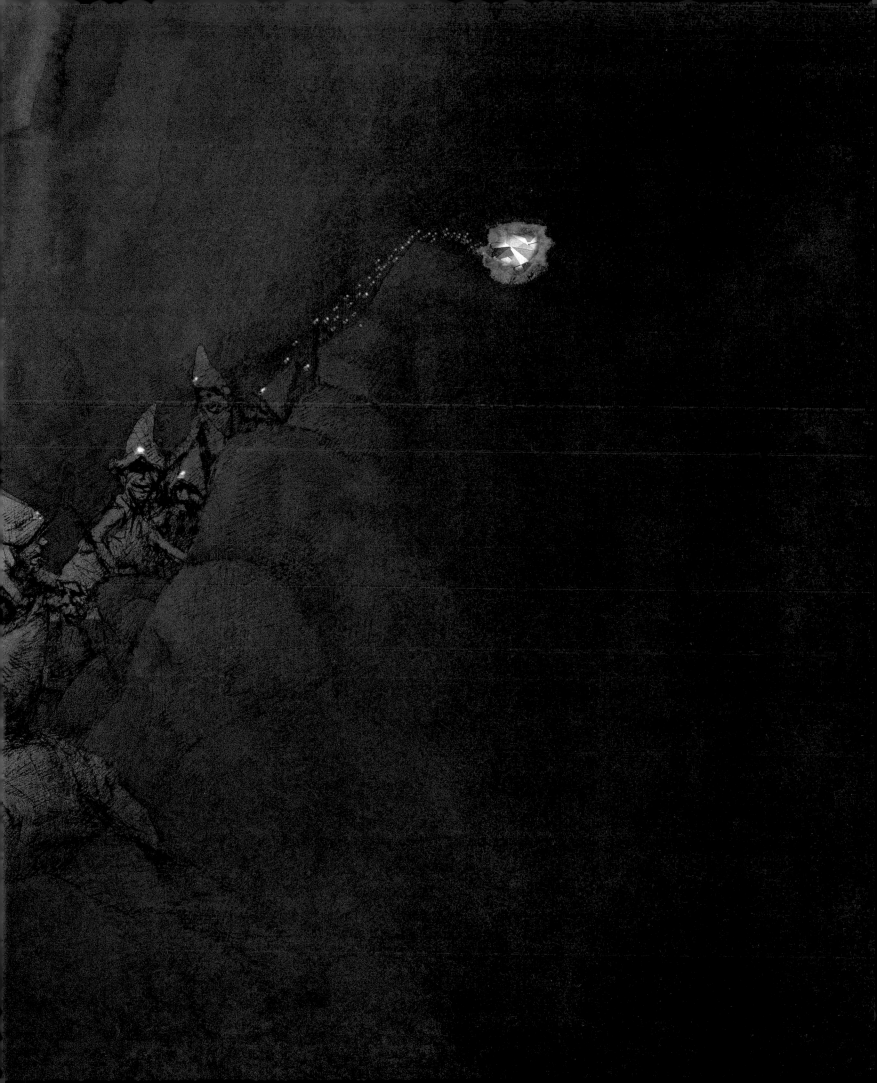

As the Crystal King appeared, Pico wanted to hide his ugly face, but the dwarves didn't give him any time.

"Tell us a story!" they begged. "The crystals from the mountain are beautiful, but they can't speak to us. You can make up stories and poems! Please. Please."

Pico was moved by their request. He sat down and began telling them a story...

Many stories later, the king said with a smile, "To say thank you, we would like to give you something." The king broke off a piece from the huge crystal and offered it to Pico.

"The magic crystal possesses a very special power," the king explained. "Anyone who looks through it sees things in their true light. Look inside, Pico, and know how you really are..."

Slowly, the dwarves lifted the crystal to his eyes. Just like a mirror, Pico saw his reflection. From the inside out, Pico's reflection was so colorful and bright that you didn't notice his humped back or ugly face.

"We hope that you will come and visit us again soon," said the king as he waved good-bye.

The crystal dwarves took Pico back to the entrance of the cave and said good-bye.

As Pico walked home, he turned the crystal in his hands and watched the colorful lights dance across the rock. The stinky old troll appeared. "What's that?" he asked suspiciously. Excitedly, Pico told the stinky troll all that had happened to him in the crystal cave.

The stinky troll looked at the crystal with greedy eyes. "Why didn't you ask for the whole thing?" complained the troll. "We could have smashed it into a thousand pieces and sold them. Then we would be rich!"

"What for?" smiled Pico. "I have friends now.
What more could I want?"

The stinky old troll grumbled to himself as he toddled off. He had to have more!
Night after night the stinky old troll lay in front of the crack in the cliff. With the next full moon, the crystal dwarves appeared and began to dance and sing.

"The magic crystal catches the eye.
It sparkles and glows like the sun in the sky."

Suddenly, the stinky old troll jumped up and shouted, "Rye! Spy! Fly high!" He thought a lot of rhyming words would have to be better than just one. The singing stopped. Surprised, the crystal dwarves stared at the rude, stinky troll. Then they grabbed him. "You must come to the king!" they shouted angrily.

The stinky old troll gladly went with them, since he believed that he would be rewarded three times as much for three rhymes! When they came into the crystal cave, the troll looked around greedily.

"I most definitely want the big one over there," he said, and pointed to the magic crystal. "And you could also fill up a sack with the smaller crystals over here," he motioned.

"Not so fast!" announced the king. "What do you have to offer us?"

"I've already given you three words," hissed the stinky old troll, "and now I want my reward!"

"Don't worry, you'll get your reward," the king replied. He broke off a piece from the magic crystal and gave it to the stinky old troll.

"Take it and see how you really are. Now go! And don't return here ever again!"

The stinky old troll was angry with the stupid crystal dwarves.
They only gave him a single, small magic crystal for his three rhymes!
Maybe he would steal Pico's crystal and sell them both…

When the stinky old troll came to the pond in the woods, he curiously
lifted his crystal to his eye and looked through it at his reflection.
He shrieked at what he saw. His insides were as dark and scary as the
throat of an old dragon! The stinky old troll ran off in shame and
disappeared deep into the forest.

Little Pico, however, lived happily. He didn't hide from other people anymore, and he made many new friends. At every full moon, Pico visited the crystal dwarves in their cave.
He danced and sang with them and then he sat down next to the magnificent magic crystal and told them all of the fascinating stories he had heard in the big, wide world outside...